THE
PINK PANTHER BOOK

BY LINDA PRESTO

ILLUSTRATED BY DARRELL BAKER

GOLDEN PRESS • NEW YORK
Western Publishing Company, Inc., Racine, Wisconsin

This city is just too hot and noisy for a Pink Panther, but I know what to do—I'll go camping.

Ah, yes, this is the life!

Aha! I see footprints! Just my size, too.
I do believe I'll follow them.

This seems to be a very long trail.
I think I'll stop right here
and catch myself some supper.

Not bad for a first try. . . .

Better. . . .

Well done, if I do say so myself!

It's a good thing I planned ahead.

Now for the tent. . . .

That's beautiful—a canvas castle. And
it's ready just in the nick of time, too.
It's starting to rain.

Lucky thing I brought this along. You never know when you might need an umbrella.

Well, this is unexpected—but delightful.
I've always wanted a water bed.

Well, it's clear I can't stay here.

Whoops!

Now, this is a lovely place to sleep.
I'm just like a bird in a cozy nest.

What's that? You don't allow sleeping in trees in this park? Then I guess I'll have to come down.

You're quite right, Mr. Park Ranger, sir.
If you'll kindly give me a hand with this
stuck zipper, I'll be on my way. I know
just the place for me.

Ah, peace and quiet. This is the place
for a Pink Panther. I'm so glad I thought
of this.